This is a work of fiction. Names, characters, places, and incidents either are the product of the author's imagination or are used fictitiously. Any resemblance to actual persons, living or dead, events, or locales is entirely coincidental.

Copyright © 2021 by StoryOlogy

All rights reserved. No part of this book may be reproduced or used in any manner without the written permission of the copyright owner except for the use of quotations in a book review. For more information, address: bedtimestriesx@outlook.com.

Book design by StoryOlogy

For my husband, the man who taught me to forgive easier, let go of anger quicker and live for today.

Forever yours, S.

Table of Contents

Introduction 4

Don't be held back 7

Outside the box 11

Encouragement 16

The Fishman and the Baker 19

Reborn 22

The Void 26

One day I'll live 33

Repetition 37

The Two Trees 40

Get him out 43

The Surprise 48

The Angry Man 51

Eyes 54

The Discarded 58

Three Wishes 63

Karma 73

An arsonist has ruined my life 80

Parent and child 90

Fin 94

Introduction

I have (maybe) like you dear reader, been angry for just about anything; ecstatic, depressed, elated, sad, scared, worried and just about every other emotion going throughout my teenage and young adult life.

Before meeting my husband, I was quite an angry person, for normal child-related issues I guess, maybe stemming from my perfect little world being torn apart when my parents divorced at the age of 11.

Throughout life, I have questioned a lot and held onto anger for as long as I could (I used to blame this on my being a Taurus). I think deep down I used anger as a cloaking mechanism, my cloak of amour if you will.

I was so used to not being the happiest person in the world that it was easier to get angry quickly and hold onto it. But what is happiness? Is it something we work towards, something that comes to us when we get older, richer, married or with more assets? Or is it something more? Is happiness internal instead of external?

Throughout adulthood, I have learnt to let go of anger easier easily whilst acknowledging that there are things I simply cannot change. I used to be a people pleaser and thought if I made everyone around me happy I would be happy. That as you may already know is not how life works dear reader.

I have now learnt to enjoy this crazy road called life more and to stop waiting for my life to start. Being rich always sounded like the dream, but as I was chasing the dream my husband used to remind me that this road that I was running down 'IS' life and if I do not start living and appreciating every pitfall, setback, hurrah, celebration and everyday chaos that is life, I may wake up one day and realise, I've missed it!

I hope you appreciate the following thought-provoking stories. Each story has a lesson to learn, enjoy.

"Limitations are but boundaries created inside our minds" Chinese proverb

Don't be held back

An adaption of - The Elephant rope.

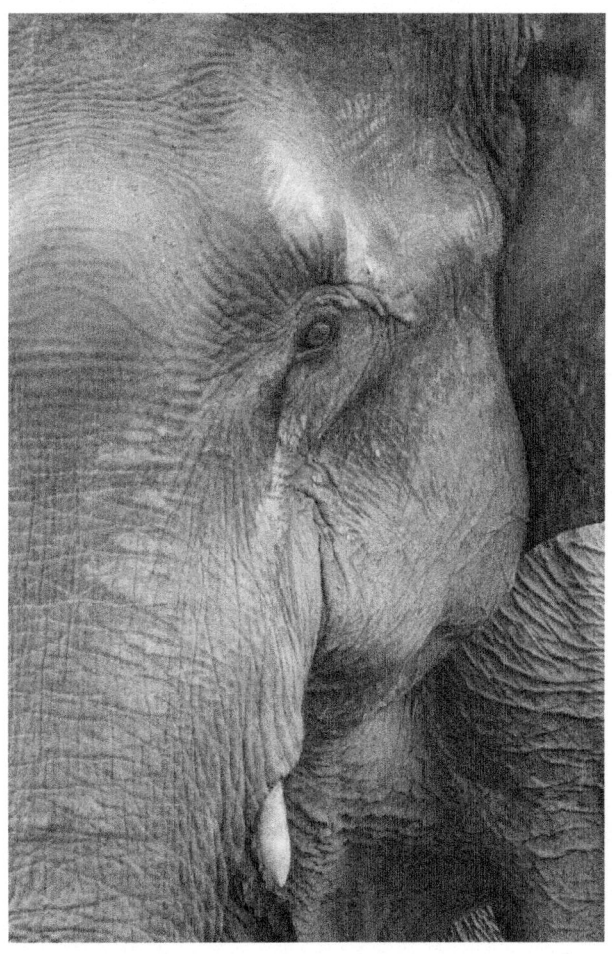

Growing up I always loved the idea of seeing the world. When I was eighteen, I packed up and flew to Greece. Since then, I have returned home five times. I am thirty-two now. A fully-fledged traveller. Travelling is the one thing I enjoy most. Meeting different people, trying new things and experiencing life is what I live for. I have not met many people like me. I meet people that want to be like me but can't.

Most people, if they had a choice, could not and would not live hand to mouth. Your average Joe wants to live my life but cannot understand how I do it. I am not rich, married, have kids or in a relationship. Don't get me wrong I have had relationships, I am just not in one now. Anyway, I digress.

The point is, for me it's simple. I work wherever I land and live there until I want to move on. Most people have the rat race life. I get it, it's the norm. Meet someone, fall in love, save for a house, purchase the house, have some kids, travel once or twice a year, build up credit, get stuff, get more stuff, compete with neighbours and friends for who has the most stuff, urgh, it never ends!

I know how I sound, but I don't care. The point is if that makes you happy then go for it. Live your life and don't hold back.

~

Last week I went to work at an elephant camp in Thailand. On my first day, I noticed the elephants all had small pieces of rope tied around their ankles. I didn't understand why. Surely the elephants could easily use their weight and with one small tug break the rope. Yet they didn't do it, they sat in their enclosures, ate when they were fed, and looked, really quite miserable, until they were allowed to go for their daily walks.

On my third day, I had quite enough and went to tell my manager I was leaving for pastures new. Before I did that though, I asked him why the elephants had the rope tied around their legs and why they didn't just break it.

His response will stay with me forever.

"When these elephants are young, we tie the same piece of rope around their ankles which they cannot move out from. We continue this daily until they are fully grown. The reason for this is to condition them to believe that they are stuck and do not have the strength to break free."

That's right. Take that message with you and don't ever hold yourself back from doing what you want in life if it makes you happy and is safe.

Moral - Believing you can become successful is the most important step in achieving it.

Outside the box

An adaption of - Thinking Out of the Box

I've always thought outside the box. I think it was my grandmother's teaching. "If life gives you lemons make a lemon cake" she would say.

We grew up poor, in a small remote village in Italy. We had little, but the love was always there.

My father always tried his best to dabble in business affairs but never really quite got the hang of being strategic with his financial planning. He got into heavy debt with a well-known, ugly, fat, sweaty, local loan shark.

He tried his best being a single parent after my mum passed. He did everything he could to bring in money, but it was my grandma who fed, clothed and taught me all I know.

One day my dad decided he couldn't continue getting further into debt and decided it was time to ask the loan shark for it to be wiped-out out of pity for us.

As he approached the sprawling white gates of the loan shark's mansion, he knew what the answer was going to be, but he swallowed his pride, wiped the sweat from his brow and proceeded to the front door.

After a short explanation from my father, and quite a few tears from him too, the loan shark fell quiet. He secretly wanted me for his wife and decided on a cunning idea.

"We will meet tomorrow on the beach, and I will place two stones from there in a bag. One white and one brown. Your daughter will pick one out.

If she picks the white pebble your debt will be wiped. But, if she picks the brown pebble your debt will be wiped and I shall have her for my wife".

Feeling disgusted with this the old man walked the three miles home, bedraggled.

Tired and depressed he explained to me what had happened. I felt sick to my stomach, but the deal was already made.

I couldn't sleep that night, and morning had arrived as quickly as night left.

The day had come, a small crowd had gathered on the beach to watch the horrific ordeal.

As the ugly, fat, loan shark bent down to pick up the pebbles I noticed he swiftly picked up 2 brown pebbles, chucked them in and closed the bag.

I had three options:

1. Open the bag and show everyone what a lying piece of pooh he was but know that we may be in trouble with his gang later.
2. Pick a pebble and marry the toad knowing my father's debt will be wiped.
Or
3. Refuse to pick any.

I swallowed nothing and reached into the bag.

Everyone held their breath.

As I pulled out one stone, I clumsily dropped it on the beach.

"Oh, my goodness, I'm so clumsy!" I said. The Loan shark turned a dark beetroot colour.

"Please don't worry, let's look in the bag and whatever is left we know which one I picked."

The shark had to play along with my game for the sake of being found out in front of everyone. He released my father from his drowning debt to a round of applause.

Moral - There is never too tough a situation that you cannot overcome. Think outside the box. Just because there may seem to be only two options, doesn't mean you can't make a 3rd or even a 4th.

Encouragement

An adaptation of - The group of frogs.

One beautiful sunny day, a group of frogs decided to go for a hop in the woods. Along the way, it started to rain. The water mixed with the earth and started to get very slippery.

They continued a short while and began hopping along faster to try and reach shelter.

Two of the frogs at the front of the group, unfortunately, fell into a deep, slippery, rocky hole, and try as they may could not make it out.

The remaining group of frogs heard their cries for help but try as they may, couldn't see a way to help the frogs out. They sadly told the two little frogs to just give up, stay in the hole, and accept their fate.

The first frog continued to jump but with the screams from the frogs above asking him not to, he realised scratching his little legs up the side of the hole was not the best thing to do. He admitted defeat and lay back accepting his impending death.

The second little frog looked at his defeated companion and then up at the screaming crowd and started to jump. With every jump, he scratched his tiny, little, bloodied legs.

The crowd was still screaming "Stop little frog", "Give up", "It's not worth it", "You'll never make it out!"

The little frog saw their shouty faces and continued jumping with all his might.

With one last almighty hop, he jumped out of the hole and landed at the crowd's feet with an exhausted thud.

The crowd gathered around him shocked and amazed "You're crazy!! Did you not hear us screaming at you to stop?".

The frog dazed and confused sat up and explained to the group that he was deaf, thanked them, and said without their encouragement he wouldn't have tried so hard to get out.

Moral - Never underestimate how powerful words are. Encouraging someone can be the difference between success and failure.

The Fishman and the Baker

There was once an old fisherman who lived with his wife in an old run-down shack. They were very poor, but they always had fresh fish to eat, a roof over their head, and a bed to sleep in. The fisherman had a deal with a local rich baker to exchange one pound of fish for one pound of bread every day.

This served the fisherman very well as he enjoyed the freshly made bread every morning and thanked God for his luck.

One day the rich, greedy baker decided to weigh the fish he was receiving as he didn't quite trust that he was receiving what they had agreed on. Upon weighing the fish, he found that the amount was indeed less than a pound. He checked every day for a week and decided to finally give the fisherman his comeuppance.

He went to the local judge with his vendetta and explained that he was being cheated out of an agreement and that the fisherman should give all his fish to him daily for five years as this was how long the contract had been going on. The judge agreed and called for the fisherman.

When the fisherman arrived in court the judge noticed how shabby his clothes were and how tired he looked compared to the fat-rich baker. He asked him if he had ever measured the fish before giving it to the baker as it was under the agreed amount.

The Fisherman replied -

"I only have one source of measurement which comes from me weighing the one pound of bread the baker gives me and then I know what one pound is."

The baker went red with embarrassment as the judge looked on, slamming the hammer down whilst saying, "As it is you who has conned the fisherman, you shall give all your freshly made bread every day for five years to the fisherman for him to resell and do as he pleases."

Moral – Don't dish out what you can't receive. Be nice always, nobody likes a nasty person and we especially don't like it when people are nasty to us. Just imagine a world where everyone was kind and nice to each other.

Reborn

There was once a bitter, racist man. It wasn't his fault he was taught not to like people by the colour of their skin by his parents. He never thought to get his own ideas as he grew up. He went through life quite satisfied but with bitter and twisted hate towards anyone who was a different colour to him. After a while, he lost his wife who couldn't stand his hatred towards others any longer and he grew old and weary.

Upon his death bed, he still held the hate within him.

After death, he awoke and found himself looking at a mirror.

~Who are you?~ The reflection asked.

"I'm John, are you God, am I God?"

~Far from it, but you have a second chance John.~

"What's that?" John queried.

~You can return to earth as a man who will become a professor, but you will not be white. Or, you could...~

"Option B," said John. "I'll choose B, anything's better than going back down there as someone who's not white." He said with a chuckle.

~Are you sure?~ said the reflection.

"Definitely," said John.

~Ok but there's a catch~ stated the reflection, ~you will remember your previous life and this conversation.~

"That's fine" chuckled John.

And with that John was reborn. John grew up to be a kind and generous man who loved and liked everyone, he was friendly and always grateful for any help he received. He remembered who he was before and the message the reflection gave him, and he promised to be the opposite of who he was in the previous life. He enjoyed being nice so much more than he expected, it felt good, it felt right.

John was reborn blind; he could not see colour anymore nor could he see anything. There was no hope either as he was born without eyes, but he lived a more fulfilled life surrounded by people of the world who he befriended through their personalities and individualities rather than their skin colour. He married, had a huge family who adored him and travelled the world. He respected all and was respected and loved by all who knew him.

Moral - Learn to see past things people cannot change or are born with. We are all human and one person does not represent a race, culture, social class, or sex. We are all equal and deserve to be treated just as you deserve to be treated.

The Void

You were on your way home when you died.

Nothing particularly remarkable.

But fatal, nonetheless.

It was a painless death.
The medics tried to save you but to no avail. Your body was so utterly shattered you were better off, trust me.
That's where you met me.
"What happened? Where am I?" You say.

You died. No point in sugar-coating anything.

"There was- there was a truck. And it was skidding."

Yes.

"I- I died?"

Don't feel bad about it. Everyone dies eventually.

You looked around. There was nothingness. Just you, and me.

"What is this place? Is this- the afterlife?"

More or less, I suppose.

"Are you God?"

Yes and no.

"My kids, my wife."

What about them?

"Will they succeed? Will they be alright?"

That's what I like to see. You just died and your main concern is for your family. That's good stuff right there.

You looked at me with fascination.

To you, I didn't look like God.

I just looked like some man or possibly a woman. Some vague authority figure perhaps.

Don't worry. They'll be fine. Your kids will remember you as perfect in all aspects. They didn't have time to grow attached. Your wife will cry on the outside but will be secretly relieved. To be fair, your marriage was falling apart. If it's any consolation she'll feel very guilty for feeling relieved.

"Oh, so what's going to happen now? Do I go to heaven? Or hell?"

Neither. You'll be reincarnated.

"Ah, so the Hindus were right?"

All religions are right in their own way. Walk with me.

You followed along as we strolled through the void.

"Where are we going?"

Nowhere. It's just nice to walk while we talk.

"So, what's the point then? When I get reborn will I just be a blank slate? Whatever I do in my next life won't matter?"

***Not exactly, everything you've experienced and learned will stay in you.

You just don't remember them right now.***
I stopped walking and put my hand on your shoulder as we reached a precipice. ***Your soul is more magnificent and gigantic than you can possibly comprehend. A human mind can only imagine a tiny fraction of what you are. It's like sticking your finger into a hot glass of water, you gain all the experiences that it had previously.***
You've been in a human for the last thirty-six years, so you haven't stretched out yet and felt your immense consciousness. If we hung out here for long enough, you would eventually start to remember all of your past experiences. But there's no point in doing that in between each life.
"How many times have I been rebirthed then?"
Oh lots. Lots and lots. This time around you'll be a Chinese peasant girl in 540 AD.
"Wait, What? You're sending me back in time?"

Well I guess, I guess time for you only exists in YOUR universe. Things are different where I come from.

"Where- Where you come from?"

Oh sure. I come from somewhere, everybody does. And there are others like me. I know you'd want to know what it's like there but you wouldn't understand.

"Oh. But wait. If I get reincarnated back in time. I must've met with myself at some point, Right? "

Sure, Happens all the time. And with both lives only aware of their own lifespan you don't even know it's happening.

"So, What's the point of it all?"

I looked you in the eye.

The meaning of life, the reason I made this universe, is for you to mature.

"You mean, mankind. You want us to mature."

***No. Just you. I made this whole universe for you. With each life you grow and mature into a larger and greater intellect. ***

"Just me? What about everyone else?"
There is nobody else, in this universe, there's just you and me.
You stared blankly at me.
"But all the people on earth?"
All you. Different incarnations of you.
"Wait, I'm everyone?"
Now you're getting it.
"I'm every human being who has ever lived?"
Or who will ever live, Yes.
"I'm Abraham Lincoln?"
And you're the man who killed him too.
"I'm Hitler?"
And you're the millions who died by his hand too.
"I'm Jesus?"
And you're everybody who followed him.
You fell silent.

Every time you victimised someone, you were victimising yourself. Every act of kindness you've done, you've done to yourself. Every happy and sad moment experienced by every human has or will be experienced by you.

You thought for a long time.

"Why? Why do all this?"

Because someday, you will become like me. Because that's what you are. You're one of my kind. You're my child.

"Wow, you mean I'm a god?"

No, Not yet. Once you've lived every human life then you will be grown enough to be born.

"So, The whole universe, it's just an egg?"

Now it's time for you to move on to your next life.

And I sent you on your way.

By Clueless - An adaption of The Egg

Moral - We have but one life, try to live it to the best of your ability. Tomorrow is not guaranteed.

One day I'll live

There was once a young girl who had a happy childhood. She was one of three sisters, had a mum and dad who were happily married, and a lovely home and friends. Towards her tenth birthday, she noticed her mum and dad arguing a lot and after a year of this, they sat her down and told her they were getting a divorce.

Her mum was pregnant with her second sister at the time and they moved far away. The girl only saw her dad once more after the move (that's when her third sister came along).

She became fixated on money as her mum was now a single parent raising three children and worked tirelessly to make them comfortable. She was the best mum and worked day and night for them all.

The girl decided that she would get rich and buy her mum a house so her mum could stop paying rent and slow down with work. Then she could finally start living, be happy and not have to rely on a man or money ever again.

She tried everything she could, buying and selling, stocks, betting, trading, manual labour, working endless jobs, and although she sometimes touched a lot of money, she never did learn to save or grow her own. Instead, she used her money to experience the things she had always wanted but couldn't along the way.

Her middle sister died shortly after she got married and had kids. She didn't grieve very well. She was very sad and wondered when she could start living her life and finally be happy.

Even though she had a family around her she had a short temper, was often moody and didn't keep a lot of friends.

She reached the age of eighty and was known as a miserable bitter woman by all who knew her, including her family.

But at the age of ninety, one of her children, who *really* didn't want to visit her, had planned a five-minute trip to pop in to see how she was. As she entered the house she noticed that her mum was singing in the kitchen and happily swaying to some music. She stayed for a further forty minutes and found that her mum was incredibly happy and in such a good mood.

The next few days passed, and the woman continued beaming from ear to ear every day. On Sunday she invited everyone over for a family dinner (something she did not do), everyone noticed that mum had *definitely* changed.

One of her grandkids even ventured up to her shyly to try and sit on her knee. The old lady scooped her up and gave her a massive kiss "I love you" she said.

"Mum" whispered her daughter from the side. "What's happened, why have you got this new lease of life and happiness?"

"Ahh," said the old lady, "I have been chasing happiness for so long I only just realised that maybe I should stop and just be happy with what I have, and then I thought about what I had and looked at all my photos and it made me so happy!"

Moral - Don't wait to live your life, we have no idea how long we have on this beautiful earth.

Repetition

Once there was a woman who had a sad life (according to her). She used to talk about her sad stories with her children constantly. She would say things in retaliation to someone saying they feel sad with "well I bet you're not as sad as me, I have sisters and brothers and none of them call me."

After a few decades, one of the daughters who was hearing one of the same stories for the millionth time turned to her and said "Mum, why do you keep going over stories of the past? Should you maybe let go and move on now?"

The mum responded that she had to go over them as that was the only way to move forward. You have to talk about these things and take things apart with a fine-toothed comb so you can be aware of who you are and who others are around you.

"Ok," said the daughter, I think I understand, I have a joke for you. As she told the joke her mum gave out a rapturous laugh.

The daughter waited for her mum to calm down and then later in the day told her mum the same joke, her mum giggled.

Just before she left she told her mum the same joke again. The mother stared at her and asked why she was repeating the joke she had already heard.

The daughter replied "It's the same as moaning or worrying. Repeating yourself doesn't do anything but waste time and energy."

Moral - Repeating the same mistakes and or stories can be a form of cloaking. You wrap yourself in a comfort blanket and believe this is what you are or what you deserve. Take the cloak off and become whoever you want to be. Only YOU can change your life and your story if you want to.

The Two Trees

Two Large trees stood next to a baby fern. The fern was only two years old and the Large trees would often poke fun at the little fern and tell it to watch how mighty they were in all weather elements.

One day a great storm came. The little fern was scared but the mighty trees laughed at the wind and the rain. "**You can't touch us for we are large, strong and old**", they boomed. The fern felt like the weather was angry and testing the trees. With every strong gush of wind and downpour of rain, the large trees stood great and tall. The little fern watched in amazement as the weather turned from bad to worse.

Now lightning had come to test the large trees. The trees stood tall and proud while the fern blew back and forth violently in the winds.

Lightning and thunder became more aggressive with every roar. The final lightning bolt struck both trees at their base and with an almighty thud, they came crashing down.

In the morning, after the great storm the two trees, lying broken on the ground, turned to look at the little fern standing upright, a little dishevelled but strong. "How is it that you stand up while we, big and mighty have fallen?" they asked.

The little fern smiled and replied, "while you were fighting the weather and standing tall, I bent and swayed with each stroke of the wind."

Moral – In life we are dealt with many obstacles. How you deal with it can be the difference between overcoming and succumbing.

Get him out

There once was an island where most people were happy and lived according to the law. The happiest were the rich who had all their greedy hearts desires. They were very comfortable knowing they were satisfied while others were not.

One day a couple were taking a nice stroll through the market when they noticed a little boy steal an apple. They were absolutely horrified and went straight up to the little boy and told the market stall keeper what he had done. The keeper shook his head and asked the little boy if he would ever do it again. The little boy said he wouldn't and started to cry but the couple were not satisfied.

They went back to their rich neighbourhood and held a meeting about the little thief. "He and his family need to leave the island; we can't have dirty filthy people like that on our island we should take them to the judge and get them thrown out" they screeched. "Hear, hear," said another.

~

The day of the trial had arrived, and all the rich, greedy, nosy residents came to watch. The couple explained the horror they saw when the boy greedily grabbed the poor market stall keepers goods and how the keeper was too afraid to tell the boy off.

The crowd began chanting "Get him out! Get him out!"

The mother of the boy then pleaded with the judge to let them stay on the island, for they were poor, had nowhere to go and he only took the apple because he wanted to let his sister taste something other than rice.

She promised the crowd she would repay every penny and more if they could simply forgive. But they did not care about forgiveness they wanted to start a divide.

If they could get this family off the island then in time they could get every poor family off too.

The judge saw the hatred, unforgiveness and greed in their eyes and could not believe that he was one of them. For he was also rich and befriended some of them, however, he also had ethics and morals from being the judge.

"I've heard enough!" The judge shouted.

"The couple *are* correct when saying the rules must be adhered to."

The mother and son wept heavily on the stand.

"It is with a heavy heart that I must side with the couple."

The crowd cheered!

"**Anyone** who has ever lied, cheated or stolen must leave the island immediately."

The judge rose to stunned faces.

He took off his robe and started walking down the courtroom towards the door.

"Where are you going" asked the couple.

"I'm leaving the island. None of us are saints and every single one of us have broken one if not all of the laws. I'll see you at the shore for the boat trip away from the island" he called as he went through the door.

Moral - For only those without sin should cast the first stone. Before we jump on the bandwagon and hate someone based on what we think we know, let us first walk a mile in their shoes before we judge.

The Surprise

Once upon a time, there was a wealthy man who loved handing out money to random people far from his home. He did this out of kindness but knew if he did this close to home his family would think him mad, and people would turn up at his door begging.

One day he went for a walk in his gardens and noticed a large stone was blocking his path. He could go round it but wanted to try something else.

He hid in the bushes and waited.

Shortly after another neighbourly king arrived for a visit. His carriage of four strong men saw the stone and went around it.

The king next saw his son and some friends come up the courtyard. They too saw the stone and if they had worked together the stone could have easily been rolled out of the path but they too continued to walk around it.

The last one to walk up the path was a lowly servant girl. She must have been no older than seventeen. The king watched in marvel as she heaved a bag of vegetables that she had just picked from one of the gardens over her shoulder and came to see the stone in the path. She placed her bag gently on the floor and slowly and breathlessly rolled the large stone away.

As she returned to pick up the bag of vegetables, she noticed a small pouch full of gold coins (the king had put it there for the person who helped move the stone to find).

The king came out of the bush and thanked the girl for her help. Relieved her from her duties and told her to go and live her best life.

Moral – Every obstacle in life presents us with a challenge to overcome. Some may not even try to overcome these challenges whilst some will see them as obstacles to overcome.

The Angry Man

There was once a very angry man who didn't have many friends or family around him, the more he got angry the more he lost people from his life which would make him angrier. Finally, he had enough, he wanted to be calmer but just didn't know how to control it.

He found an ad in his local paper for anger management and called the number. The next day he drove the forty miles to a small farm and was greeted by a kind-faced farmer who showed him to his room, told him to unpack, and advised that training would commence after.

The man was eager to know what this little old lady could do for him, so he got unpacked right away.

The farmer told him to start to talk about his life and every time he got angry to pick up the heavy nails in a bag on the floor and hammer one into the fence. As he started talking about his life he immediately got angry and started to hammer.

On day one he hammered forty nails.

Day two – twenty-five nails

Day three – ten nails

He could feel himself not wanting to hammer more and more as his therapy sessions continued although he was still angry with the people that left his life.

On Day five he hammered no nails.

"Very good," the farmer said.

"Now I want you to remove each nail every time you feel calm.

By day nine all the nails had been removed.

Feeling very pleased with himself the man began to pack. Just as he finished saying his thank-you's, the farmer told him to turn and look at the fence.

"Every nail you pushed into that fence was anger fuelled. When you say or do things in anger they leave scars like this. You can remove a dagger plunged into someone, but the scar remains."

Moral – Be careful what you say in anger. three things come not back; A spoken word, A sped arrow and A missed opportunity.

Eyes

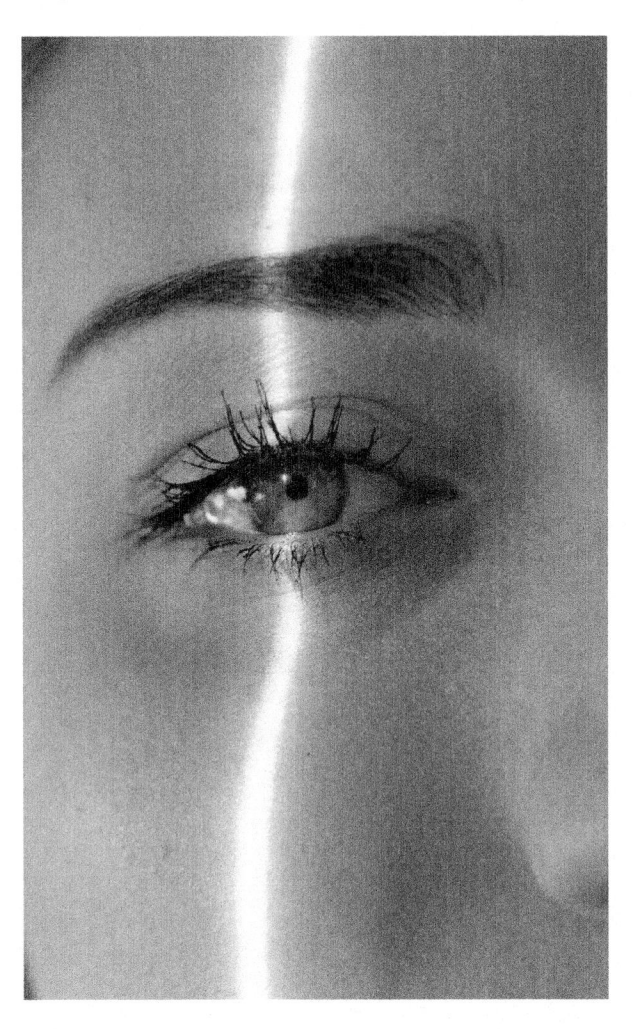

A beautiful young girl suffered a terrible accident at the age of 18 and became blind. She went through bouts of depression and hated herself.

On her twenty-fifth birthday, she sat in the park feeling sorry for herself when a stranger sat beside her and struck up a conversation.

A little while later they were walking around the park laughing and chatting. The girl felt very at ease with the man and he asked for her number.

After a few dates, they became boyfriend and girlfriend. The girl began to fall in love with the man but was still very hurt about having no sight. She mentioned it in passing every day and often said 'if there was one thing she could wish for, it would be her sight back.'

The man fell head over heels in love with her and after a year of dating asked for her hand in marriage. The girl immediately declined and told him he didn't want to marry a blind girl. "The only way I will marry you is if I can see the world again".

A few years later a revolutionary eye surgery had arrived, and the girl immediately signed up, she waited three months for a matching eye donation.

The day finally came. Matt, her boyfriend went with her for moral support.

After the surgery the girl could see instantly, she could see the world again and was so happy.

When Matt walked in she was shocked to discover he was blind. She felt betrayed that he didn't tell her and told him she could never marry someone like him.

A few days later a letter arrived through the post. She was so happy to see a letter addressed to her she immediately tore it open....

"Take care of my eyes.

I love you, Matt."

Moral – Never kick those who hold you up at the worst of times.

The Discarded

There was once a young boy named Scott with a drive for success. He was bullied throughout his primary school years and swore that he would become rich so he would be able to do what he wanted when he wanted and gain people's respect.

He worked tirelessly through school, achieved A*'s at GCSE and went on to achieve a 1st in his Finance Degree. Throughout university, he became very ruthless and heartless and only looked out for himself. His university flatmate was also a Finance student but had the complete opposite outlook to him. Where Scott was vindictive and selfish, Matt was compassionate and kind.

One day over dinner Matt told Scott about a financial opportunity to get a training programme with a Big 5 firm that was coming into the university. There was only one place, but he told Scott to apply too and wished him the best of luck.

Scott decided on a plan. A few days later he invited some of the top students from his financial class for a pizza party. Little did they know the pizzas were laced with laxatives.

The next day only 3 people turned up for the test to be taken on as a trainee for the prestigious company. Scott had eliminated most of the competition and received an offer to start as soon as he graduated.

Everything was going according to the plan. When Matt felt better he confronted Scott and asked him why he would go to such lengths to get a place.

"You can only count on yourself in this world. It had to be done and I have no regrets!" said Scott proudly.

Scott went on to be very rich, he got everything he wanted in terms of wealth and stepped on more people along the way to move up the ladder.

On his thirty-fifth birthday, Scott made a few unfortunate large investments that all turned the opposite direction through the announcement of a government breaking story, and he lost tens of millions of pounds.

He not only lost all of his wealth in one day but most of his companies too. He knew what this meant, he would be blacklisted from every company in the city probably the country.

After a stint of depression, homelessness and alcoholism, Scott decided to pick himself up and try and piece his life back together.

On his fortieth birthday, he found a shelter and bought a suit at a nearby charity shop. He was going to his first interview in over twenty years and he was quite positive about it.

He had seen an ad for a training program for people with financial backgrounds that had been out of work for over two years. It was perfect for him; he could do this, and it would help him get back on his feet.

The interview went as well as could be, Scott was feeling positive.

Scott looked at the interviewer with familiarity and asked -

"I feel like I know you from somewhere, did we hang out at the Ritz or a box in Wembley?"

The interviewer chuckled. "No Scott, it's me Matt your old Uni flatmate."

Scott felt dread. He wanted to run and never turn back.

"I erm, I'm so sorry about all that. Please don't hold that against me, I really need and can do this job".

"Please don't worry Scott," said Matt "This was an excellent interview and you definitely have the job!" "I forgave you years ago mate, holding onto anger is poison, welcome to the team!"

Moral – Treat others how you would like to be treated. You never know who could help you in the future.

Three Wishes

There was once a young woman by the name of Sara who had a nice life, but she yearned for more. Sara always looked at her friends and others and secretly felt envious that they were prettier, had more money and had a better life than her.

~

Sara decided to stop moaning, her thirtieth birthday was coming up and although she didn't have the life she had planned she would seize the day and travel by herself.

Sara booked a trip to Mexico for a trip of a lifetime. She found a single friends cruise and decided to embrace meeting new people and seeing new things.

On the first day of her holiday, after unpacking she booked an excursion around Bacalar, a beautiful small town, four hours from Cancun. On the tour, she noticed a small ramshackle hut in a nearby street with a sign above saying – 'Wishes granted here' - She excitedly asked the tour guide about it but he advised "Don't go to things like that, it's not worth it, trust me".

This piqued her interest and she told the guide she would meet the group back at the meeting point later in the day.

Upon entering the shack, she was greeted by a very warm and friendly old woman who told her to hold out her palm.

Sara did as she was told, and the lady advised that she would give her three wishes.

'This is bloody hilarious' she secretly thought but went along with it anyway.

"Ok, so are there any non-wishes?"

"Not at all" the old lady replied, "but I must warn you, be careful what you wish for, it might come true".

She thought long and hard about what her first wish should be then had the perfect answer.

"Well, obviously I wish for more wishes" she queried.

"Your wish is my command," said the old lady.

"Is that it, what happens next?" said the woman

"Well, you wished for more wishes so you can keep going."

"Riiiight," said the woman "Ok I wish for one million pounds!"

"Your wish is my command," said the old lady.

"Where is it then?" asked the woman.

"Your wish will be granted when it is ready," said the old lady.

"OOOOkaaaaay!" Said the young woman sarcastically. And with that, she up and left.

The remainder of the trip was lovely but on the last day, she received a call from her dad telling her that her mother was in a car crash and was in the hospital.

The plane ride home was exhausting. She spent the next four days with her father at her mother's bedside until the very end.

The funeral was as to be expected, and the young woman fell into an eternal pit of sadness. A few days later her father called to ask if she could come over and hear her mother's last will and testimony.

Sara was to inherit her mother's London home (which she bought before marrying her dad and let out for extra income), and all her jewellery. A total value of one million pounds.

She felt nothing and just wanted her mum back.

A few months later she picked herself up and decided life had to move on.

It was a random Sunday, as she was brushing her teeth it suddenly hit her! The old lady in Mexico told her that her wish for one million pounds would arrive when it was ready, then her mother dies and the estate she receives is valued at £1 million!

She booked the next flight to Mexico.

Once she had settled into her hotel she went straight out to find the old little shack.

As soon as she walked in the little old lady was sat in the same position with what looked like the same clothes as before with the same smile. The woman tearfully explained what she had wished for the last time she was there, that shortly afterwards her mum had died, and then she had inherited an estate valued at £1 million!

The old lady looked at her with confusion. "But you got what you wanted, why are you so sad?"

"NOT LIKE THIS!!" Screeched the woman "If you had told me that someone had to die for me to get it I would never have wished for it!"

"You did not specify how you wanted the money and the universe does not work like that."

Exasperated, the lady held her head in her hands and started to sob.

"You have plenty more wishes" whispered the old lady. "If I remember correctly, your first wish was for more wishes"

Sara sniffed and looked up. "Can I go back in time and un wish for the £1million so my mum is alive?"

"There are no rules," said the old lady "You just make a wish but be careful, it might come true".

Sara thought long and hard. This time she would make sure she got it right! Her mum is all she wanted in this world and that was worth more than any amount.

"Ok," she said.

"I wish to go to before I found this shack when my mum was alive, and I did not ask for £1 million please."

"Your wish is my command." said the old lady with a cheeky smile.

"Is that it? Are you conning me? This isn't funny." she screamed at the old lady.

Sara got up, left the shack, and walked to the end of the road. Where she saw her tour guide and joined him.

~

She noticed a small ramshackle hut in a nearby street with a sign above saying – Wishes granted here - She quickly asked the tour guide about it, but he advised "Don't go to things like that, it's not worth it, trust me".

This piqued her interest and she told the guide she would meet them back at the meeting point later in the day.

Upon entering the shack, she was greeted by a very warm and friendly old woman who told her to hold out her palm.

Sara did as she was told, and the lady advised that she would give her three wishes.

'This is bloody hilarious' she secretly thought but went along with it anyway.

"Ok, so are there any non-wishes?"

"Not at all" the old lady replied, "but I must warn you, be careful what you wish for, it might come true."

She thought long and hard about what her first wish should be then had the perfect answer.

"Well, obviously I wish for more wishes" she queried.

"Your wish is my command," said the old lady.

"Is that it, what happens next?" said the woman

"Well, you wished for more wishes so you can keep going."

"Riiiight," said the woman "Ok I wish for one million pounds!"

"Your wish is my command," said the old lady.

(She stayed in this loop for ten years before she was let out)

Moral – Be careful what you wish for – It might come true in the most unexpected way!

Karma

There was once a young woman who was quite bad and selfish throughout her teenage years. She stole, lied, and only thought of herself. She grew up and still held the same selfish ideals but learnt to be civil and fake and grew up to marry and have kids. She forgot about all the trouble she had caused in the past and never apologised for it.

As her children grew so did hers and her husband's bank account. She was happy (in public) and loved showing off every time she bought something new for the house or herself. She had a group of friends who were kind of like her and she relished keeping up with the Joneses.

At night she would drink wine and smoke secretly in the garden, for inside she wasn't as happy as she thought she was.

One day she was shopping when she bumped into an old school friend. She immediately tried to say sorry and walk on for she didn't want to be seen with someone that was not of her level.

"Hi Sarah," said Becky.

Sarah sighed and turned around with the biggest grin.

"Oh, hello how are you?" replied Sarah.

Becky went on to explain that she was great had 3 kids and just moved into the area.

'Oh great' thought Sarah exasperatedly.

"We should catch up some time," said Becky, and they made a date to have dinner.

'Screw that' Sarah thought as she left the exchange and blocked Becky's number.

A few months passed and Sarah was becoming more bored with her life. She loved the attention she received when people entered her home and commented on how fabulous it was as well as her hair, bags, clothes, shoes, and new perfume but deep down something was missing and she didn't know what.

Her husband had returned from a business trip one day, dropped his bag in front of the washing machine and ran up for a shower (as he normally did). As Sarah started to unpack his bags she noticed a strong smell of women's perfume but brushed it aside as she knew most of the women he worked with and none of them could compete with her in looks, plus they all worked together so it made sense that he could smell like one of them.

A few months passed and Sara bumped into Becky again outside a charity shop.

"Hi, Sarah!" Said Becky happily.

"Oh hello" replied Sarah fakely.

Becky didn't mention the last meeting that Sarah didn't turn up to but offered a playdate with the kids so they could hang out. Sarah responded and accepted the invitation.

A few days later Sarah bought her kids to Becky's house for a playdate. She intended to come up with an excuse 10 minutes in and leave the kids for the hour, go for a sauna then pick them up at the end but when she drove to the house, she saw that Becky's house was twice the size of hers, she instantly hated her.

As she was given a grand tour around her house she grew green with envy.

"Oh, I'm so sorry," she said reaching for her phone as she was shown the swimming room.

"It's my mum, she needs me to pick something up for her, would you mind if I leave the kids here and run and help her".

Becky accepted with a smile and told her to take all the time she needed.

Upon leaving she noticed a red cufflink that looked familiar on the side table in the hallway but thought nothing of it.

At the Spa, she heard some of her high society friends talking about the new lady that had moved into the manor house. They were discussing if they should invite her to one of their fundraisers.

'Absolutely not' thought Sarah and she glided over to them and explained that Becky was not the type of person they wanted at her party. She made up a lie that she was a slut and slept with married men.

The women immediately alienated Becky from their social scene.

A few weeks later the two old acquaintances bumped into each other again. Becky inquired as to why the other woman were ignoring her and Sarah played to her naivety. She advised that they were just snooty and to stick with her own friends for they didn't even compare.

Many months later Sarah continued on her quest to alienate Becky from her social scene. One day Becky approach Sarah (after learning what she had done from an acquaintance).

"I'm sorry but you don't belong here" Sarah reasoned "I just don't associate with people like you so please just go find your own friends".

Becky stared at Sarah for the longest time and with a sigh said "You know when I first moved here I found out your husband was cheating with someone close in your circle, that was after I moved here to be near him not knowing that he was married to you. My children's father is your husband. After meeting you I wanted to sit down and tell you face to face about what an arse he was but then you just blanked me and have been mean ever since. For no reason. Karma is a bitch"

And with that Becky walked off.

Moral – Apologise for your transgressions. Karma can bite in many ways.

An arsonist has ruined my life

I was eight when our home caught fire. I remember standing on the other side of the street, staring in awe as black smoke curled from the top of the windows. My mother was bawling her eyes out as a neighbour wrapped a blanket around my shoulders. My father just stood there, arm around my mothers' waist with a blank look in his eyes. He had worked so hard to provide us with a good home and it was burning down in front of him. All our earthly possessions, the family photos, and the heirlooms were feeding an unforgiving inferno. By the time the fire trucks arrived the roof was starting to collapse. The firefighters didn't even try to save our home, it was a total loss. They worked to stop the fire from spreading to the trees and neighbouring homes as the dry August wind started to carry the embers.

I was fifteen when part of the school caught on fire. I watched from three blocks away. We had moved to a new town shortly after our last home burnt to the ground. From the front porch, I could see the school just down the road. The red-hot glow illuminated the dark clouds and cast the trees in orange light. Soon the flashes of cold blue and white strobes joined the warm colours radiating from the gymnasium. All our neighbours were outside watching the same show. Their excited and worried chatter was almost as loud as the sirens. The school district brought in mobile classrooms for us to attend, it was well over a month before we were allowed back into the actual building.

I was eighteen when the convenience store on the other side of town caught fire. The black smoke rolled across the noontime sky and filled the neighbourhoods with the stench of burning plastic and processed food. The firefighters battled the flame for hours and in the aftermath discovered the store owner blackened and curled in a foetal position where the office once stood.

I was twenty-two when the woods caught on fire. I decided to go camping by myself in southern Oregon. I needed some alone time to clear my head from the pressures of college. I had just set up my tent a started a small campfire when I saw the red light glowing from the other side of a large hill. I stared in disbelief for longer than I should of. Birds and small woodland creatures started working their way through the trees, running past me. Soon I saw deer, wolves, and a few bears also running away from the hill. I turned and started to run as I saw the first flames flicker above the crest. I left my camping supplies as I booked it towards the road. The raging fire illuminated my path as the sun dipped behind the distant mountains. After what seemed like an hour of panic and desperation, I could see flashing lights through the forest. First responders grabbed me took me to the hospital where I was treated for smoke inhalation and questioned by police. I learned later that while they couldn't decern the exact cause of the fire they did discover four hikers who didn't make it out.

I was twenty-five when the local Catholic church burst into flames. I watched from my office as fire poked through the steeple and licked the cross. The heat caused the surrounding trees to burn and fill the sky with rolling grey smoke. The fire department wasn't able to save the structure or the three people who had been unlucky enough to be trapped by the heat.

I was thirty-two when the local hospital burned to the ground. It was a small and outdated hospital that was in the process of shutting down as a new, and much larger one had been built on the edge of town. This small hospital still treated minor conditions and housed several doctor offices. The fire was deemed as a wiring issue. Seven janitors, one radiologist, and a clerk died that night.

I was thirty-eight when the homeless shelter caught fire. The shelter had stood for a long time and had helped many people over the years, offering them a temporary home, resources, and food. The managers and volunteers had enough time to evacuate everyone before the flames claimed the building. The authorities later declared it an act of arson and they suspected some of the homeless people. Not enough evidence could be collected to determine anyone's involvement though.

I was forty-one when the dealership went up in smoke. Stacks of tires burned hot and filled the sky with oily black smoke. Vehicles began to catch fire before the fire trucks could roll in. They fought the blaze for hours as I watched from my apartment. My fiancé complained about the smell and hopped out loud that no one was hurt. The sheriff made a statement about their suspicions of arson.

I was forty-three when I lost another home to a freak fire. I was out of town for a business meeting when it happened. The fire had started in the kitchen of our ranch style house and spread at a horrific rate. The entire house was engulfed in less than fifteen minutes. My wife and baby daughter were both asleep when it started. The neighbours could hear their screams as they burned. The investigators decided that this was caused by an arsonist. They put out an emergency warning to the township that someone in the community was a pyromaniac and a serial killer.

I was forty-five when the arsonist struck again. A low-income apartment building was set on fire. I saw the orange glow in the night sky as I was walking to the liquor store. I diverted and got close enough to watch the action. Firefighters attempted to rescue as many people as they could but in the end, eighty-seven inhabitants died. The fire had been started in both entrances to the building with an unknown accelerant. The Sheriff called on the FBI to aid them in their investigation since they couldn't find a solid lead. Federal agents stayed in town for several weeks before giving up and moving on.

I was forty-seven when my place of employment burned. Having lost my comfy office job thanks to my drinking, I ended up as a security guard at the local tire factory. It was three minutes past midnight when the alarms started. I quickly made all the necessary phone calls according to the procedure. The fire had started in the warehouse and thankfully the overnight workers managed to make it out unscathed. The fire raged white hot and it took the fighters two days to put out the blaze. This fire was also accredited to the mystery arsonist. Unfortunately, I was brought in for intense questioning as a suspect. Eventually, I was cleared of all potential guilt.

I was fifty-two when some of the homes in my trailer park raged with burning heat. These fires were automatically associated with the arsonist. One of the trailers held an unknown meth lab and it exploded. Shrapnel from the lab punched through nearby homes. By morning thirteen people had died from the fire and the explosion.

I was fifty-four when the rate of man-made fires started to increase. At least once a month some building was burning in town. People were moving out at an alarming rate, fearing for their safety and that of their families. The police chief was running ragged, trying to get ahead of the situation. The FBI kept making regular appearances as they were trying to figure it out.

I was fifty-four when the grain elevator exploded. The arsonist hit during harvest season when the silos were full of corn and dust. The police had marked the elevator as an obvious target and managed to catch a photo of the maniac.

The man was covered from head to toe in black clothing, but it was the first lead they had.

I was fifty-five when the cops knocked on my door with questions. Questions that when answered, landed me as a suspect once again.

I am now fifty-nine, I have been sitting in prison for three years now. One smart cookie of a federal agent had connected the right dots. He realized that I had started all those glorious fires and had gathered enough evidence to pin the crimes on me. Only after I was found guilty by a jury of my peers did I fully admit to my involvement. Ever since my first camping trip with my dad I have been obsessed with flame. The fire calls to me and fills me with joy. Its mesmerizing flicker transports me to a place of mental clarity. The power of its purifying heat calms and soothes my soul. I obtain a feeling of power and control and the blaze washes over the lives of others. If there is a god, he is fire and smoke. I'm told I will die here in this prison, never to have freedom again.

I'm ok with never leaving this prison. But they're mistaken if they think they can keep me away from the fire.

By Brokenwrench

Moral – Be careful who you befriend. Not everyone is as they seem!

Parent and child

There once was a poor father who adored his little girl. Christmas was coming and he tried desperately to get her a doll she had seen in the toy shop window one day. Although he worked back to back shifts he didn't have enough money to spoil her. He could not justify getting just the doll and them not having Christmas food for the holidays, so he bought a cheaper doll and some Christmas food for them to enjoy.

When he got home that night he was annoyed at himself for not being able to afford what she wanted and continually snapped at her for doing normal 3-year-old things. The last straw was when he came back from cooking dinner and noticed the girl had used all the roll of wrapping paper he had just bought to wrap her Christmas present. After scolding her about how much things cost and to think before she acts the little girl began to cry and said she was just trying to wrap a present for him.

He immediately felt guilty and apologised for his outburst, tucked her into bed and went to sleep.

On Christmas day they had a lovely breakfast together. The father had to wrap the doll in plastic bags as he had no wrapping paper and repeatedly said sorry to her as she was unwrapping it. When she saw the doll she screamed with excitement, kissed the doll, and kissed her dad.

The dad, feeling overwhelmed, felt guilty again and was angry with himself for not appreciating that he had such an amazing little girl.

When it was his turn to open his present the little girl sat, doll in arm, excited for the big reveal. When her father opened the box and noticed nothing inside he started to get worked up again. "Don't you know there should be something inside the box when you give it to someone as a present?" The little girl got very upset and explained that she had filled the box with kisses just for him.

The dad again felt terrible and gave her the biggest hug. "I love you" he whispered.

A few months later he lost his little girl to a life-threatening disease.

The father takes out an imaginary kiss from the box every year on her birthday and vowed to never again be angry over silly things and to remember what is important in life in memory of his beautiful daughter.

Moral – Appreciate the little things in life, for they are the big things. Things you can buy can be replaced, get boring and go out of fashion. Love lasts forever.

FIN

To finish on this story was debatable, but I think it is one we all need to read and feel. We all go through times where we want to buy the best gift or even all the gifs our loved ones want, even if we can't afford it. We get annoyed easily when we are stressed out or busy. We are human, it happens.

We have to try and remember what we are here for and what the main point of it all is.

Love is the best present of all. Things come and go, get destroyed, break, get replaced, go out of fashion and so on but Love will never die.

Being the best version of ourselves is not easy otherwise we would be doing it right now. Being angry or sad is often easier than taking a risk and being happy. Some of us get so comfortable with being sad that it's frightening to try and be happy just in case we get sad again.

We have to take each day as it comes. If our time was up, right now how would we feel? Have we lived a fulfilled life, did we do all we could to make ourselves and others happy? Can we forgive ourselves for our past transgressions and try to live a better life for our future?

A quote by Lao Tzu:

"The journey of a thousand miles begins with one step."

To start the new chapter of our life we need to make a change today.

Remember that; live along the way, enjoy life as it is not guaranteed, and try to enjoy and provide as much passion, kindness, and love as you can.

Just imagine a world where everyone was kind, understanding and accepting.

Thank you for reading, I hope you enjoyed it.

Volume 2 out soon.

Printed in Great Britain
by Amazon